For Oliver de Lecq Marguerie
S.H.

For Tom
R.C.

Text copyright © 1993 by Selina Hastings
Illustrations copyright © 1993 by Reg Cartwright

First U.S. edition 1993
First published in Great Britain in 1993 by Walker Books Ltd., London.

Library of Congress Cataloging-in-Publication Data:

Hastings, Selina.
The firebird / retold by Selina Hastings : illustrated by
Reg Cartwright.—1st U.S. ed.
"First published in Great Britain in 1993
by Walker Books Ltd., London"—T.p. verso.
Summary: A retelling of the Russian folktale in which a young
huntsman and his wise and magical horse are ordered by the king
to undertake a series of increasingly difficult tasks.
[1. Fairy tales. 2. Folklore—Soviet Union.] I. Cartwright, Reg, ill.
II. Zhar-ptitsa. III. Title.
PZ8.H265F1   1993
398.2—dc20   [E]   92-52997
ISBN 1-56402-096-7

10 9 8 7 6 5 4 3 2 1

Printed and bound in Hong Kong

The pictures in this book were done with oil paints.

· Candlewick Press
2067 Massachuetts Avenue
Cambridge, Massachusetts 02140

Retold by
SELINA HASTINGS

Illustrated by
REG CARTWRIGHT

CANDLEWICK PRESS
CAMBRIDGE, MASSACHUSETTS

There was once a strong and mighty king whose power extended far beyond the boundaries of his realm. This king was a tyrant whose wish was his command, to be instantly carried out, no matter how difficult, no matter what it cost in time or trouble. In his prime he had been a great warlord, and there was no man in the kingdom who was not, in his secret heart, afraid of him.

Now the king had one servant whom he valued above all the rest. This servant was a huntsman, a young man who was brave in the field and true to his master. He worked hard because he enjoyed his work, and also because he wished to advance in the world. He often dreamed of having a wife and a little house of his own to take the place of the lonely room over the stables in which he lived at present. The huntsman had a horse who was as valiant as he—and, it must be said, a good deal wiser.

One sunlit autumn morning, riding along a grassy path that led through the middle of the forest, the huntsman saw something gleaming gold and partly hidden in the fallen leaves. Dismounting, he bent down and saw that what had caught his eye was a feather, a feather that shone bright red and gold like a tiny tongue of flame.

Just as he was about to reach down for it, his horse spoke. "That is a feather of the Firebird. Do not, I beg you, pick it up. For if you do, trouble such as you have never known will fall upon your head." The huntsman hesitated. But then he thought what a magnificent present it would make for the king, and how well rewarded he would be as a result. So he ignored his steed's advice and picked up the feather.

The king, like most men in his position, was difficult to please. He was, however, delighted with his present—so delighted that he said to the huntsman, "Since you have found the Firebird's feather, you must now bring me the Firebird. I am determined to possess her. And if you fail in this, I shall strike off your head with my sword."

Horrified, the huntsman went to find his horse. "You said trouble would come, and come it has. What am I to do?"

"Oh, this isn't trouble," said the horse consolingly. "The real trouble still lies ahead of you. This is nothing.

"What you must do now is ask the king to have one hundred measures of corn spread over an open field before dawn tomorrow."

The king gave the order, and it was done.

The next day at dawn the brave huntsman rode to the field, set his horse loose, and hid behind a tree to keep watch.

At first it was too dark to see anything, but as the light grew and the first rays of sun crept over the meadow, there was a sudden rustling and sighing as the forest trees bent this way and that, and with a beating of wings the Firebird alighted on the field, her lovely feathers gleaming, her golden beak greedily pecking up the corn. Silently the horse came up behind her and stepped firmly on one of her wings, while the huntsman appeared with a rope with which he quickly bound her.

The poor bird, struggling and frantic, was helpless, and the huntsman soon had her back at the palace and delivered to the king.

The king was beside himself with pleasure. He stroked his beard, which was thick and coarse and which every morning he had oiled and scented. He congratulated the huntsman for his cleverness in securing such a rare prize. "It appears that there is nothing you can't do!" said the king. "So, as you have captured the Firebird, you can now get me a wife.

"At the very edge of the world, where the red sun rises, lives the beautiful Princess Vasilisa. Bring her to me, and I will reward you with more gold and silver than you have ever seen in your life. But if you fail, I shall strike off your head with my sword."

The huntsman was dismayed and went weeping to the stables where his horse was kept. The horse spoke soothingly. "This isn't trouble. The real trouble lies ahead of you still. This is nothing.

"What you have to do now is ask the king for a silken tent with a golden top, enough food for a feast, and some of the best wine in his cellars."

All this was easily procured. The huntsman rode to the edge of the world where the red sun rises from the blue sea, and there he saw in the distance the Princess Vasilisa skimming over the water in a boat with silver sails. He unharnessed his faithful horse and set him free to graze before pitching his tent and spreading temptingly in front of it the provisions he had gotten from the king.

Soon the princess noticed the golden top of the tent glinting and gleaming in the sun, and her curiosity was aroused. "Whatever can that be?" she wondered, and turned her little boat toward the shore.

As she walked toward him, the huntsman bowed low. "Welcome, Princess. Will you come and sit with me, and allow me to offer you a glass of wine?" The princess, who was very young, had never tasted wine before, but she liked the look of this young man and thought no harm could come of just one sip. Deeply moved by the lady's beauty, the huntsman carefully poured her a large goblet of the royal wine. The wine was the color of rubies and it tasted of rose petals, and before she knew it the princess had drained her cup.

The wine mounted to her head, and soon she fell fast asleep.

The huntsman gazed adoringly down at her for several moments before picking her up and laying her tenderly across his saddle. Then he rode as fast as he could away from the edge of the world and back to the palace.

The king, who was robed in velvet, his beard freshly oiled, his person perfumed from the top of his head to the soles of his feet, greeted his bride ecstatically. She was even lovelier than he had heard. There was nothing he would not do for her, and little that he would not give to the faithful servant who had brought her to him. He conferred upon the huntsman a dukedom, vast estates, and a fortune that would support him and his descendants in luxury forever.

But Vasilisa, awaking appalled to find herself in an unfamiliar place, burst into tears. Not quite daring to tell so powerful a king that she would rather die than marry him, she made up her mind to make it as difficult for him as she could. "Deep at the bottom of the sea lies a great stone," she sobbed, "and under that stone my wedding dress is hidden. Without that dress I will not wed!"

The king sent for the huntsman. "You must return at once to the blue sea, and bring back the gown that lies hidden under a stone. If you succeed, I will reward you more richly than before. If you fail, I shall strike off your head with my sword!"

Wretched at the misery of the lovely princess, but frightened, too, for his own skin, the huntsman went at once to find his horse. Again the horse was reassuring, patiently explaining, as before, that this was not the trouble, that the real trouble still lay ahead, that this was nothing.

The two of them returned to the seashore, and there, deliberately, the horse stepped on a crab. The crab squealed out in terror. "Please, please don't kill me! Spare my life and I will do whatever you wish!"

"What we wish," said the horse, his hoof still on the crab's shell, "is for you to bring us the Princess Vasilisa's dress, which lies under a stone at the bottom of the sea."

"It shall be done!" cried the crab, and scuttled away.

Within minutes the sea began to tremble and seethe as

hundreds of crabs, big and small, swam to the surface and crawled out onto the sand. They listened carefully to the instructions of the first crab, whose life was so distressingly at risk, and then turned and crawled crabwise back to the sea.

For a full hour the huntsman and his horse kept their eyes fixed on the water. Nothing seemed to be happening. Then all of a sudden the surface of the sea was boiling with crabs, their claws hooked into a dress that they were dragging up from the deep.

The huntsman, weak with relief, rode as fast as he could to the palace.

But Vasilisa turned pale when she saw what he held in his hands. Now what could she think of to put off her wedding to the king?

"I cannot marry you," she said desperately, "unless you give the command for the young man who brought me my dress to bathe in boiling water!"

The king hesitated for only a moment. It was his favorite servant he would be sending to his death, but what did that matter if Vasilisa would agree to marry him? He ordered a cauldron of water to be fetched and set on the fire and, as soon as he saw steam rising, had the huntsman brought before him. "Now this *is* trouble," said the huntsman to himself. And kneeling to the king, he asked him if, as a final favor, he could say farewell to his horse. The king agreed to his request.

So the huntsman went for the last time to his horse. "Yes, this is trouble," said the faithful animal. "But do not be afraid. I have the power to help you once more." And summoning all his strength the horse cast a spell over his master to protect him from the boiling water.

The huntsman stood before the king. At the word of command six members of the palace guard seized him and threw him into the cauldron. The princess gasped and covered her face with her hands. Even the king closed his eyes— only to open them again a few seconds later to see the huntsman smiling and unharmed in the boiling water. Not only that. As he climbed out of the bubbling pot everyone saw to their astonishment that the young man, who should by now have been dead, had turned into a youth of almost supernatural beauty.

The princess stared, enthralled. Never had she seen such a handsome man. "If only he could be my husband," she said to herself. The king, too, was impressed by the transformation.

"If only I could look like that," he thought, "then Vasilisa would marry me at once." And he tore off his velvet cloak and plunged into the water.

Of course he was boiled to death at once—and no one pretended to be sorry, least of all Vasilisa and the huntsman.

As soon as the king had been buried with the respect due to his rank, the two of them were married, and on the same day the huntsman, by popular acclaim, was crowned.

He never forgot to whom he owed his life and fortune, making sure that his horse always had everything he wanted. And just occasionally, when faced with a problem difficult to solve, he would take off his crown and creep down to the stables for advice.